Wish Upon a Party

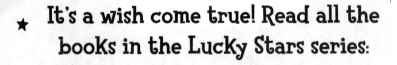

It's a wish come true! Read all the books in the Lucky Stars series:

Wish Upon a Party

by Phoebe Bright
illustrated by Karen Donnelly

SCHOLASTIC INC.
NEW YORK TORONTO LONDON AUCKLAND
SYDNEY MEXICO CITY NEW DELHI HONG KONG

With special thanks to Maria Faulkner

With thanks to all the magical people
in my life for their belief in me

ISBN 978-0-545-42001-3

12 11 10 9 8 7 6 5 4 3 2 1   12 13 14 15 16/0

Printed in China   68
First Scholastic printing, October 2012

Lucky Star that shines so bright,
Who will need your help tonight?
Light up the sky, and thanks to you
Wishes really do come true. . . .

Hello, friend!

I'm Stella Starkeeper, and I want to tell you a secret. Have you ever gazed up at the stars and thought that they could be full of magic? Well, you're right. Stars really are magical!

Their precious starlight allows me to fly down from the sky. I'm always on the lookout for boys and girls who are especially kind and helpful. I train them to become Lucky Stars — people who can make wishes come true!

So the next time you're under the twinkling night sky, look out for me. I'll be floating among the stars somewhere.

Give me a wave!

Love,

Stella Starkeeper

1

The Great Fandango

"Snap!" said Cassie, putting a matching card on the pile in front of her. "I'm going to win this time."

"We'll see about that," said Alex. He grinned and put down another card.

It was a rainy day in Astral-on-Sea. Cassie and Alex were playing a card game called Snap in her bedroom at Starwatcher Towers. Cassie's parents owned the Starwatcher Towers Bed and Breakfast, and Alex was her new friend. He was staying there on vacation with his parents and his little white puppy, Comet.

"SNAP!" Alex shouted. "That's two wins for me and one for you. You see, it's all about probability."

"*Probability?*" Cassie repeated.

"It's a theory scientists use to figure out how often something might happen," Alex replied. "I'm figuring out how often the cards will come up in pairs by counting the cards in between."

Cassie smiled. Of course Alex would come up with a scientific way to play Snap!

"I think you're just lucky!" she said.

She looked up at the glass roof of her bedroom and sighed. It curved around into a dome shape like her dad's observatory. At night, Cassie liked watching the stars through the glass, but now all she could see were raindrops falling in a steady *pitter-patter*.

"It's raining too hard to go outside," she said, petting Twinkle, her old black cat. He purred happily. "What if someone's making a wish? How will I know, if I'm stuck inside?"

"You already helped make three people's wishes come true," Alex pointed out. "So the probability is good that you'll help a fourth person."

Twinkle nuzzled Cassie's arm, and the charms on Cassie's bracelet tinkled together. Stella Starkeeper, Cassie's magical friend, had given her the silver bracelet for her seventh birthday a few days before. Every time Cassie helped make someone's wish come true, she received

another charm with a new magical power!

So far, she had four charms — the bird charm made her fly, the crescent moon let her speak to animals, and the butterfly charm helped her freeze time. Her newest charm was a purple flower, but she didn't know what its magic power was yet. When she earned seven charms, she would become a real Lucky Star, just like Stella. Then she would be able to grant any wish she liked! But Cassie knew she had a lot to do before that magical day.

Cassie looked up at the gray sky again. There was no sign of Stella Starkeeper among the clouds.

She heard Alex's stomach growl loudly. "I'm hungry," he announced.

"I'm hungry, too," Cassie agreed, giggling. "Let's go and get some breakfast."

Cassie carried Twinkle downstairs to the dining room. He sat under the table near Cassie's feet while she and Alex ate some soft-boiled eggs and toast.

"I wonder if it will ever stop raining," Cassie said with a sigh.

"Hi," a new voice interrupted. "I think I can make your gray day disappear!"

Surprised, Cassie turned to see who had

spoken. A boy stood in the dining room doorway. He was a little taller than Alex and wore a black cape. He gave them a goofy grin. Cassie recognized him as one of the new guests at the bed-and-breakfast.

"Hi!" Cassie said. "I'm Cassie, and this is Alex."

The new boy bowed. His shiny black cape swung around his shoulders, revealing a bright-red lining.

"I am The Great Fandango," he announced in a booming voice.

"That's a very unusual name," Alex said, grinning.

"My real name's Marcus Chen," the boy told them, sitting down. "The Great Fandango is my stage name. I chose *Fandango* because it sounds magical, and *Great* because that's what I want my tricks to be."

"You're a magician!" Cassie said excitedly.

Marcus nodded proudly.

"I'm going to be a scientist," said Alex.

"Wow," Marcus said, "that's *great*, too."

Cassie and Alex laughed.

"Why do you have your magician's outfit on now?" Alex asked.

"I'm doing a magic show at my cousin

Lia's birthday party," Marcus explained. "She's turning five today. I don't see her very often because we live far away, so the magic show is my birthday present to her."

"What a fun idea!" Alex said.

Cassie and Alex grinned at each other. They knew a lot about magic, because of the magical adventures they had with the charms on Cassie's bracelet.

"We love magic," Cassie added.

With a flourish, Marcus pulled out a black wand with a white tip. "Then I'll show you my magic tricks," he said.

He turned the bottom half of Alex's empty eggshell upside down on a plate. Then he shook out a clean napkin and carefully covered the empty shell.

As she watched Marcus, Cassie noticed a glimmer of sunshine peeking through the dining room window. *This could turn out to be a magical day after all,* she thought with a smile.

2
Magic Tricks

Marcus slowly waved his wand over the napkin and tapped it three times. *Whoosh!* He whipped the napkin away.

All three kids looked at the eggshell. Aside from a small crack, it looked exactly the same.

"Oops," Marcus said.

"Is something supposed to happen?" Cassie asked.

"There should be a new egg in its place," Marcus explained.

He tapped the egg again. Nothing happened.

"I guess the yolk's on me," he said, shrugging.

Cassie and Alex giggled.

"Try another trick," said Cassie. "You just need to keep practicing."

Marcus nodded. "The Great Fandango never gives up!" he cried. He pointed his wand at the scarf that Cassie wore. "Would you mind if I borrowed your scarf?" he asked.

"Not at all," Cassie replied. As she untied the scarf and gave it to Marcus, the silver moons on it sparkled.

"I'll place the scarf up my sleeve. And when I wave my wand, the scarf will multiply to make one hundred scarves!" Marcus explained.

He waved his wand in the air, then reached inside his sleeve. He frowned slightly.

Oh, boy, Cassie thought. *The trick's gone wrong again. Poor Marcus.*

Marcus looked up his sleeve and slowly pulled out . . . Cassie's scarf!

"That's weird," he said. "It's supposed to be a string of scarves all knotted together."

Then he lowered his arm—and a plastic egg dropped out of the sleeve!

Marcus opened his eyes and mouth wide, making the funniest surprised face, and Cassie and Alex burst out laughing.

"Well," he said, "at least
I found the egg!"
Cassie giggled.
"You're so funny!"
"But I'm not a
very good magician,"
Marcus said sadly.
"I have lots of
practicing to do
this morning
if I'm going to
make Lia's birthday
party special."

He gave a bow, swirled his cape, and
walked out of the dining room.

"I'd better get going, too," Alex said.
"It stopped raining, and I promised to

take Comet for a walk. Do you want to come?"

"I should help Dad wash the guests' breakfast dishes," Cassie replied. "But I'll see you later."

"Okay," Alex said, waving and heading off to find his puppy's leash.

Down by her feet, Twinkle meowed loudly at Cassie. It was as if he was trying to tell her something!

"Ooh, just a minute, Twinkle." Cassie concentrated hard on the crescent moon charm on her bracelet. After a minute, silver sparkles swirled around the bracelet and her furry cat.

"Now I can understand you," said Cassie. "What were you saying, Twinkle?"

"That boy is funnier than a dog chasing its tail!" Twinkle meowed.

"Marcus is funny," Cassie agreed. "He really wants to be a magician, but he keeps getting his tricks wrong." She looked at her pretty flower charm. "I wonder if my new charm could help him."

"I think he'll need a lot of help," Twinkle said, batting the plastic egg under the table. "But I like him even if his tricks don't work."

"Me, too." Cassie smiled as she piled the breakfast plates onto a tray. She had just picked up the last plate when she spotted a dazzling streak of light stretching across the sky outside the window. A shooting star!

Twinkle spotted it, too, and bolted under one of the dining room chairs.

"Dad," Cassie called into the kitchen, "can I go out and play now?"

"Of course," her dad replied. "Thanks for your help."

Cassie ran outside, following the spinning star down the hill toward the apple orchard.

With a *whizz* and a *fizz* and a *zip-zip-zip*, the star zoomed over the orchard. Then it slowed and hovered by one particular tree. Cassie watched as it grew into a column of dazzling light, which slowly changed into Stella Starkeeper!

Wearing a glittering dress, a sparkling jacket, and shiny leggings, Stella sat on a branch swinging her silver boots back and forth.

"It's so good to see you," Cassie said, scrambling up the tree and giving Stella a big hug.

"You've been very busy," Stella said, touching the new flower charm on Cassie's

bracelet. "You earned your fourth charm already. Good job!"

Cassie beamed, feeling very proud.

"Only three more charms to earn, Cassie, and then you'll be a Lucky Star—just like me," said Stella. She tapped the little flower charm. Cassie gasped as the charm transformed into a whole bunch of flowers before becoming a single flower again.

"How did you do that?" Cassie asked, her eyes wide.

"I'll give you a clue," Stella said with a wink. "Sometimes things appear out of thin air."

Then, in a cascade of glittering sparkles, she disappeared.

Sometimes things appear out of thin air, Cassie thought. *What does that mean?*

3

Disappearing Magician

"Cassie!" a familiar voice shouted.

Through the trees, Cassie saw Alex walking up. Comet was scampering nearby on the end of his leash.

"Hi," Alex said, running over. "Your mom asked if we would pick up the cupcakes she ordered from the Fairy Cupcake Bakery."

"Oh, good," Cassie said, scrambling down from the branch. "Maybe we'll see Kate there." Cassie's friend Kate often helped her mom make the cakes and cookies at their bakery.

Cassie, Alex, and Comet walked down the hill and along the waterfront. Cassie peered around, trying to spot someone who might need her help. There were lots of people walking along the boardwalk, and there were kids on the beach building sand castles and splashing in the waves. Everyone looked perfectly happy, enjoying the sunshine after the morning rain.

I don't see anyone who might need to make a wish, she thought.

When they reached the bakery,

Cassie took a
deep breath.
The air was
filled with the
amazing smell of cakes and cookies!

"Comet, I think we'd better wait outside,"
said Alex.

As she pulled the door open, Cassie

couldn't help laughing at the little puppy, who was gazing longingly through the bakery window.

Inside, the shop bustled with people buying the beautiful pastries, cookies, and cakes that lined the shelves. Cassie could see Kate and her mom busily serving the customers from behind the counter.

Cassie joined the line behind a cheerful-looking lady carrying lots of bags and boxes.

"I'm here to pick up a birthday cake," the lady said when it was her turn. "It's for my daughter, Lia. She's turning five today."

Cassie realized that the lady was Marcus's aunt! *The cake must be for his cousin's party*, she thought, *where Marcus is going to do his magic show.*

"Oh, Mrs. Chen," Kate's mom said, "you're a little early, so I'm afraid it isn't quite ready yet."

She pointed to a beautiful pink and white cake covered in yummy icing. There were five star-shaped silver candles on top. A marzipan fairy castle sat next to the cake, along with some sparkly fairies made from sugar.

"The icing has to set completely before the fairy decorations can go on," Kate's mom explained.

"I understand," Mrs. Chen said, looking

flustered. "But I have so many things to do for Lia's birthday party that I don't know when I can come back."

Cassie knew just what to do!

"Excuse me," Cassie said. "My name's Cassie. Marcus is staying with us at Starwatcher Towers, and he told us about Lia's party. Maybe my friend Alex and I

could pick up the cake for you. I could ask my mom to bring us in the car."

"Oh, that's very nice of you, Cassie," Mrs. Chen said. "Are you sure your mom won't mind?"

"I'm sure," said Cassie. Her parents were always offering to help the guests at the B&B.

"Thank you so much," said Mrs. Chen. "Would you and Alex like to come to the party? It's in the garden at the Flashley Manor Hotel."

"We'd love to, thanks!" Cassie replied, but inside her heart sank. *I hope Donna Fox doesn't try to ruin Lia's party*, she thought. Donna's parents owned Flashley Manor, and Donna liked to get her own way.

Kate had finished helping the other customers, and now ran over to Cassie with a box of cupcakes.

"They're beautiful!" said Cassie, peeking inside the box. The cupcakes were decorated in swirls of yellow, orange, and green icing and topped with shiny cherries.

"Mom put in a few extra cupcakes for you and Alex," said Kate as she closed the pretty box. "Give her a great big thank-you for us," Cassie said. Waving good-bye to Kate, she ran outside and joined Alex and Comet.

"We have to go back and pick up Lia's birthday cake later," she said. "I volunteered to help. And look—Kate's mom gave us some extra cupcakes!" She lifted the lid of the box.

"Yum!" Alex said. "They look delicious."

Comet yipped excitedly.

"He thinks so, too." Alex laughed.

"Let's bring a cupcake to Marcus," Cassie said.

"Great idea," Alex agreed. "We can find out how his magic tricks are going."

Cassie held on tightly to the cupcake box as she and Alex ran back up the hill to Starwatcher Towers, Comet yipping the whole way. They picked out the extra cupcakes to share with Marcus, and left the rest on the kitchen table.

But where *was* Marcus?

They searched all over Starwatcher Towers. He wasn't in his guest bedroom or in the living room, dining room, or kitchen. They even checked Cassie's dad's observatory and her own bedroom at the top of the house. But there was no sign of Marcus anywhere.

"It's almost like he magically disappeared!" Cassie said.

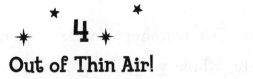

4

Out of Thin Air!

Cassie and Alex sat on the front steps of Starwatcher Towers, wondering where to look next. Twinkle was dozing in the sunny flower bed. Comet licked the old cat's ear, and Twinkle opened one sleepy eye.

"Twinkle likes to watch the guests coming and going," Cassie said. "Maybe he knows where Marcus went."

She concentrated on her crescent moon charm. Silver sparkles swirled around her bracelet—and around Twinkle, too!

"Twinkle, have you seen Marcus?" asked Cassie.

"I think he went to the apple orchard," Twinkle replied. "He almost tripped over me because of all the boxes he was carrying. I had to move off the front steps."

"Thanks, Twinkle," Cassie said, giving the cat a tickle under his chin.

Leaving Comet in the garden to play with Twinkle, Cassie and Alex ran to the orchard.

Just then, Cassie had a great idea. "It'll be easier to spot him if we fly," she said.

She took Alex's hand and thought about the bird charm on her bracelet. Silver sparkles danced around them both . . . and their feet lifted off the ground. *Whoosh!* Together, they flew up over the trees.

Suddenly, they heard a dramatic voice below them cry, "Abracadabra!"

"I think we've found him," Cassie said, nudging Alex.

Looking down through the trees, she spotted Marcus standing on a stage. It was made of the wooden boxes that her parents used to collect juicy apples! He was using another crate as a table, with a shiny black box on top. Behind Marcus, an old sheet hung between two trees to create a backdrop. Poking out from under the sheet was a colorful bag full of magic props.

"I don't think we should interrupt him," Cassie whispered. "It looks like he's trying a really difficult trick."

Cassie concentrated on her bird charm again. The silver sparkles swirled around them as they dropped gently from the sky and landed behind a tree.

As they watched, Marcus picked up a squishy apple from the ground and held it in the air.

★　✳　★　✳

"Ladies and gentlemen," he said, pretending he had an audience, "for my next trick, I will turn this apple into an orange!"

With a flourish, he tapped the shiny black box three times and threw the apple into the air.

"Abracadabra!"

Cassie held her breath. Would the trick work?

Splat! The rotten apple came down on Marcus's head. Though he did look funny covered in squishy apple, Cassie held back her laughter.

"Oh, no," Alex whispered. "His trick went wrong again."

Cassie knew she had to do something. She ran out from behind the tree, with Alex close behind.

"What a cool stage, Marcus!" Cassie said.

"It looks great," Alex added.

"Thanks." Marcus grinned. "If only my magic act was great, too." Just then, the side of the black box dropped open and an orange rolled out. "Oops!" he said. "That was supposed to happen earlier."

Cassie and Alex laughed.

Marcus laughed, too, but then he sighed. "I can't get any of my tricks right," he said. "Lia's going to be so disappointed. I wish I could make her birthday party special."

Cassie and Alex shared a secret glance. Marcus had made a wish, and it was up to

Cassie to make sure it came true! On her wrist, the little flower charm twinkled in the sunlight.

I need to find out what power this charm gives me, she thought. *Then I can help!* She knelt to pick up the orange and turned to Marcus. "You'll make Lia's birthday special. You just need some practice."

"Really?" Marcus asked.

Cassie nodded. She looked over at Alex, who seemed to be frowning in concentration.

"And we'll help you, won't we?"

"Of course," Alex replied. Suddenly, he snapped his fingers. "In fact, I have an idea for a new trick! All we need are three cups big enough to hide a cupcake!" He held a cupcake out to Marcus.

"But I don't have any cups," Marcus said. "Only magic tricks."

Both boys looked glumly at the bag of props.

"I can go and find some in the B&B," Cassie offered. "Be right back!"

Cassie jogged up the hill to Starwatcher Towers and searched the kitchen cabinets. On one of the shelves she spotted two large mugs.

These would be perfect, she thought. *But I need three of them! If only an extra mug would appear.*

Without thinking, she gazed at the flower charm on her bracelet. The flower glittered . . . and then changed into a bunch of flowers! Silver sparkles swirled around the bracelet and over the kitchen counter. *Poof!* With a little burst of stars, a third mug appeared— out of thin air!

★ ✳ ★ ✳

"Wow!" Cassie breathed, remembering what Stella Starkeeper had said earlier. "So that's what my flower charm does—it makes things appear. That's the perfect kind of magic to help a magician!"

5

Where's the Cupcake?

Cassie ran back to the orchard. She could hear Alex saying something to Marcus.

"Whatever you're talking about sounds very scientific," Cassie said, laying out the mugs next to the cupcake. They were exactly the right size!

"I'm explaining the theory of probability to Marcus," Alex said.

"Isn't that the theory you used to win Snap?" asked Cassie.

"That's right," said
Alex.

Marcus scratched his
head. "I don't understand it."

"I think you'll have to
show us, Alex," Cassie said.

"Okay," said Alex,
nodding firmly. "I can
show you with
the cupcake
trick."

Alex hid the
cupcake under
one of the mugs, turned
the other two over, and slid
them around on the table in figure eights.

"Now guess which mug the cupcake is under," he said.

"The one on the right," Cassie said.

"No, the left," Marcus cried.

Alex lifted the two mugs—but the cupcake wasn't under either of them!

"Look!" he said, lifting the middle mug to reveal the cupcake.

Cassie and Marcus clapped.

"Most people will *probably* guess the left or the right," Alex told Marcus. "There's a two-thirds chance they won't pick the middle mug. So you have to make sure the cupcake always ends up in the middle."

"Very clever," said Cassie.

Alex showed Marcus how to do the trick. "Now you try," he said.

While Marcus moved the mugs around, Cassie pulled Alex behind the curtain.

"I figured out what my flower charm can do," she said. "Watch this."

Cassie concentrated on her flower charm. It burst into a bunch of flowers, and sparkles swirled around her bracelet. *Poof!* A shiny green apple appeared in her hand.

"That's amazing!" said Alex. His mouth hung open.

"Maybe I have to make something appear

out of thin air to help Marcus," Cassie
suggested.

"Maybe," said Alex thoughtfully. "But
what?"

Just then, Marcus called, "I think I've got it!"

Cassie and Alex ran to watch. Marcus moved the mugs so fast that they had no idea where the cupcake was when he stopped.

"It's under the mug on the left," Cassie shouted.

"No, it's on the right," Alex said.

"You're both wrong," Marcus said triumphantly. With a flourish, he lifted the middle mug. But the cupcake wasn't there.

"Oops," he said.

"Try again," said Cassie with a smile.

Marcus tried the trick a few more times, but he just couldn't get it right.

"Oh, well," he said, disappointed. Then he brightened. "Hey, when I *do* find the cupcake, I know a trick that will make it disappear completely."

Once again, Marcus
moved the mugs around
and around—and
again he lost track of
the cupcake. When
he finally found it, he
plucked the cherry off
the top and ate the rest!

"See?" he said. "It disappeared!"

Cassie and Alex almost fell over laughing.
Marcus grinned and stuck the cherry on the
end of his nose, making them laugh even
more.

"Marcus, your tricks might go wrong, but
you really know how to make people laugh,"
Cassie said. "And that's a special kind of
magic."

Marcus frowned. "But I promised Lia that she'd get to see some real magic tricks," he said gloomily.

"Don't give up," Cassie said. "Lia will love your show. You're a magician *and* a comedian, all in one!"

"Besides," Alex piped up, "I figured out a way for you to remember where the cupcake is." He showed them a tiny chip on one of the mug handles. "If you always place the cupcake under the chipped mug, you'll know exactly where to find it."

Marcus tried the trick again with another cupcake under the chipped mug. It worked!

Finally, they packed up the stage and the props, and headed back to Starwatcher Towers.

"Well, I'm as ready as I'll ever be," Marcus said. "It's almost time for Lia's party. I just hope I can remember my tricks with everyone watching."

Whatever happens, Cassie thought, *I have to make Marcus's wish come true. Lia's going to have the best party ever!*

Her mom came downstairs and grabbed her car keys. "Your mom and dad are already at the party, helping set everything up," she explained to Marcus.

"I told them I'd drop you off."

Cassie, Alex, and Marcus piled into the car with Cassie's mom. On his lap, Marcus held his bag of props—including a cupcake!

Their first stop was the Fairy Cupcake Bakery, to pick up Lia's birthday cake.

"It's beautiful!" Cassie told Kate's mom when she saw the pink and white cake with the fairy castle and sparkly fairies on top.

"Lia's going to love it!" said Marcus.

Cassie helped her mom place the large cake box in the back of the car for the drive to Flashley Manor Hotel. Cassie hoped it wouldn't wobble around too much. She wanted it to be perfect for Marcus's cousin!

A few minutes later, Cassie's mom dropped them off in front of the hotel. Cassie and

Marcus carefully carried the cake up the sweeping steps to the large front door, with Alex behind them, ready to catch the cake if it fell.

As they reached the top step, the door flew open and a girl wearing a sparkly leotard and leggings glared at them.

Cassie's heart skipped a beat. It was Donna Fox!

6
A Magic Show

"Who invited *you?*" asked Donna.

"We brought Lia's birthday cake for Mrs. Chen," Cassie said, holding the cake box out in front of her.

Cassie took a step back as Donna's blue eyes narrowed. "And what are *they* doing here?" Donna asked, pointing to Alex and Marcus.

"Helping," Alex mumbled.

"Marcus is Lia's cousin," Cassie added.

★　✳　★　✳

"Otherwise known as The Great Fandango. He's going to do a magic show for Lia's party."

"The Great Fandango, huh? We'll see if you're so great," Donna snapped. "Just remember, this is the great Flashley Manor

Hotel, and it belongs to my parents." With a flick of her ponytail she turned and marched ahead of them. "The party's back there," she said, pointing through a white and gold door.

"Thank you," Cassie said politely, but Donna was gone.

Carefully, Cassie, Marcus, and Alex carried the cake down the thickly carpeted hallway. It led to a grand room with velvet-covered furniture and twinkling chandeliers hanging from the high ceilings. But the party was supposed to be in the garden!

"Donna sent us the wrong way," Cassie realized with a sigh. Donna Fox was so awful sometimes!

At last, they found the shiny glass doors

that led out to the garden. Cassie's heart lifted
when she saw a sparkly banner strung across
the trees that read, *HAPPY BIRTHDAY,
LIA!* in big letters. Lots of kids were playing
on the lawn and there were brightly colored
balloons everywhere.

Cassie and Marcus placed the cake on a
table next to a platform with a red curtain
across it.

"Look, Marcus," Alex said. "This must be
the stage for your magic show."

Marcus's mouth dropped open. "I really hope I don't get my tricks wrong in front of everyone," he said. He waved to his mom and dad, who were talking to some of the other parents.

Just then, Mrs. Chen came hurrying over. "Hi, Marcus! It's so nice to see you." She kissed his cheek. "And, Cassie, thank you so much for bringing the cake."

Cassie and Alex smiled. It was turning into a great day!

I'm sure I can grant Marcus's wish now, Cassie thought.

Marcus carefully placed the cupcake and the mugs for his trick on the table, next to the cake box.

"Could you bring these props onto the

stage when I do the cupcake trick?" he asked
Cassie.

"Of course," she said.

"Maaaaarcus!" squealed
an excited voice.

"Lia!" he cried,
as a girl with
long black
braids ran
across the
lawn and threw
herself into his
arms. He grinned
and spun her
around.

"It's my birthday," she said, her eyes
sparkling. "I'm five!"

"I know!" Marcus grinned. "Happy birthday."

"And Mom says you have a special birthday treat for me," she whispered, pointing at the stage. "I'm so excited, I might burst!"

Cassie, Alex, and Marcus laughed.

At that moment, Mrs. Chen clapped her hands. "Could all the kids come and sit in front of the stage, please?" she called. "We have a special birthday treat for Lia — a magic show!"

"Hooray!" Lia cried. "I can't wait to see Marcus's tricks!" She settled down in front of the stage with her friends.

"Good luck," Alex told Marcus.

"You'll be great," Cassie added. "After all, you're The Great Fandango."

Marcus grinned again and went behind the curtain to get ready.

Cassie and Alex joined the other kids to watch the show. Cassie could feel butterflies fluttering in her stomach. She felt nervous for Marcus.

If anything goes wrong, Cassie thought, *I'll find a way to help him. I have to make sure his wish comes true!*

"Ladies and gentlemen, girls and boys," announced Mrs. Chen, "please welcome The Great Fandango!"

She pulled a cord and the red curtains swept open to reveal Marcus in his magician's

cape and hat. Everyone cheered — and Lia
was the loudest of all! Marcus bowed.

"For my first trick . . ." he began.

But a screeching voice interrupted. "I want
to do my acrobatic act!"

Cassie looked around to see Donna Fox
marching out of the hotel and toward the
stage. Her parents were right behind her.

"But, sweetie, they have an act already,"
Donna's father said.

"You promised," said Donna, her voice
rising.

"Yes, of course," her mother agreed. "Mrs.
Chen, would you mind letting Donna do her
act first?"

"Of course she doesn't mind," Donna said.
"I'll be amazing."

With that, she leaped onto the stage, doing cartwheels and somersaults. She didn't pay any attention at all to Marcus, who scooted out of the way in surprise.

Poor Marcus, thought Cassie. *Donna is such*

a show-off! I have to stop her from ruining Lia's birthday.

Cassie stood up. But she was too late! Donna cartwheeled right into one of the poles that held up the stage curtain. It toppled sideways onto the cake table, dragging the curtain with it.

Squish! The beautiful fairy-castle birthday cake was flattened — and so was Marcus's cupcake.

Lia burst into tears. Up on the stage, Donna took a bow. Cassie saw her give Marcus a smug little smile. His act was ruined.

If only Donna had been splattered with icing, Cassie thought angrily. *Then she wouldn't look so happy with herself!*

To Cassie's amazement, her flower charm

started to tingle, then
burst into a bunch of
flowers. As Donna
skipped past the table,
the squished birthday
cake plopped onto the
ground by her feet,
sending up a spray
of gooey icing. It
covered Donna's
costume and
face in sticky
drips! She shrieked
in horror.

Oh, wow! Cassie thought.

All of the kids burst out laughing, even
Lia. Cassie couldn't help thinking that

Donna looked pretty
funny covered in sticky
icing. But then she saw
Marcus in his
magician's cape and
hat, looking sad.

This is terrible, Cassie thought. How am I
going to help Marcus now?

★ 7 ★
Magical Birthday Party

Furious, Donna pushed her way past Marcus and stomped into the hotel, with her parents close behind. Cassie walked over to Marcus, who was holding Lia's hand.

"I can't do my magic show," he said, showing Cassie the squished cupcake. "Sorry that you can't have your birthday surprise now, Lia."

"Thanks anyway, Marcus," Lia said. "I'm just happy you came to my party."

Cassie thought about how brave Lia was trying to be, even though she was disappointed. Then Cassie looked over to where Mrs. Chen was clearing up the mess made by the ruined birthday cake—and she had an idea.

Maybe I can make Marcus's wish come true after all! she thought.

"Marcus," she said quietly, "you can still do your magic show."

"But how will I do the ending without the cupcake?" he whispered.

Cassie looked around and spotted Alex helping set up the lucky dip game. He was pulling the last little gift out of a box covered in silvery paper. Under the table she saw the empty box from the Fairy Cupcake Bakery, and a striped box that had held the balloons and banner.

"Just leave the ending to me," she said brightly. "I promise it will work out!"

Marcus still looked worried.

Cassie straightened his black cape. "Remember, The Great Fandango never gives up," she said gently.

Cassie headed over to pick up the cake box and the striped box, then joined Alex.

"Can I borrow this?" she asked, pointing to the silver box.

"Of course," Alex said, shrugging. "What are you going to do?"

"A very special probability trick," Cassie replied, winking.

She and Marcus climbed up onto the stage. With some help from Mrs. Chen, they managed to hang the red curtain back on the pole.

"Ready?" Cassie whispered to Marcus.

He nodded.

"Can you all take your seats again, please?" Mrs Chen called to the kids. "The Great Fandango is ready continue his magic show now."

Lia and her friends cheered. Cassie watched from behind the curtain as Marcus started

his show again.
Soon, everyone was
rolling with laughter.
Marcus lost the
scarves in the scarf
trick again, and
then produced
a dozen eggs
from his sleeve

while clucking loudly like a chicken.

The kids clapped and roared with laughter.

"Boys and girls," Marcus announced, "that's almost the end of my magic show."

Everyone groaned.

"But I have one last trick," he said. "Do you want to see it?"

The whole audience cheered.

Marcus walked over to Cassie. "What do I do now?" he whispered as she passed him the three boxes.

"You're going to make a birthday cake appear under one of the boxes," Cassie replied.

"I am?" Marcus said. He looked awfully nervous all of a sudden.

"You're The Great Fandango," Cassie reminded him. "All you have to do is believe in birthday magic."

Marcus nodded and turned back to the

audience. "Boys and girls," he said. "For my final trick, I will make a birthday cake appear in one of these boxes." Everyone oohed and aahed as he placed the cake box upside down on the stage, then put the striped box and the silver box on either side of it.

I hope this works, Cassie thought, crossing her fingers.

"I need a volunteer from the audience," Marcus said, pointing to Lia. Smiling, she jumped up onto the stage.

Marcus handed her his wand. "Please wave the wand over the boxes," he said.

Lia did, looking thrilled to help with a magic trick.

"Now choose the box you think the cake is in," Marcus said.

Lia picked up the silver box. Her face fell. "There's nothing there," she said.

Marcus opened his eyes wide in a funny surprised face, tossed the box in the air, and made it land on his head like a crazy hat. Lia giggled.

Next, Lia picked the striped box. Nothing was under that one, either.

Marcus reached slowly toward the cake box. Behind the curtain, Cassie concentrated hard on her flower charm. *Please make a*

beautiful birthday cake appear, she thought. Silver sparkles swirled around her bracelet, and she felt a tingling sensation go up her arm.

On her wrist, the flower charm burst into a bouquet!

Marcus picked up the cake box, and the audience gasped. There was a beautiful cake underneath! It was topped with a fairy castle and sugar fairies, just like before, and sparkled with edible glitter.

Lia's eyes shone. "Oh, Marcus, thank you!" she cried. "You're the best. And this is the best birthday ever!"

"Hooray!" Cassie cheered along with everyone else. Then she felt a tingle on her wrist. With a swirl of shimmering stars, a beautiful cupcake charm appeared on her bracelet. She had done it! She had granted Marcus's wish—he had made Lia's birthday extra-special with his magic show. And now Cassie had earned another magic charm!

"You're the greatest magician in the world," Lia said, hugging Marcus tightly.

"You really are," Mrs. Chen said, joining them. "I have no idea how you did that trick, Marcus. Where did the cake come from?"

Marcus looked at Cassie.

She raised an eyebrow. "A great magician never reveals his secrets," she said.

"I don't know how it happened, either," added Marcus, "but it goes to show that if you believe in magic, anything is possible."

★ ★ ★

That night, Cassie floated up through the open panel in the glass roof of her bedroom. Silvery sparkles spiraled from her bird charm and swirled all around her. In her hand, she held a gift for a special friend.

The sky was filled with stars, but Cassie flew straight toward the star that glowed the brightest of all. As she got closer, it grew even brighter and then changed into Stella Starkeeper.

"Hi, Stella!" said Cassie, waving. "Look,

I've got a new charm!"

She held up her wrist so Stella could see the colorful cupcake charm on her bracelet.

"I'm so happy to see that," Stella said. Her eyes sparkled. "You only have two more charms to earn. Then you'll be a Lucky Star!"

Cassie sighed. "I can't wait," she said. "But I can't quite control my magic yet. I accidentally covered Donna Fox in icing!"

Stella gave Cassie a hug. "It isn't easy becoming a Lucky Star, but I know you can do it."

"I brought something for you," Cassie said, "to thank you for always believing in me."

She held out a cupcake, all the way from the Fairy Cupcake Bakery. On the top, in bright pink icing, were the initials *SS*—for Stella Starkeeper.

"Delicious," Stella said, taking a bite.

"It's magical, just like your new charm!"

Cassie looked at the little cupcake charm on her bracelet.

Whose wish will I grant next? she wondered. *And what magical adventures will I have?*

Make Your Own!

Cassie loves cupcakes! She gets delicious cupcakes from the Fairy Cupcake Bakery, and she even has a cupcake-shaped charm on her bracelet. Now you can make some yummy Lucky Star cupcakes for yourself!

You Need:

- Your favorite cupcake and frosting recipes, and all of the necessary ingredients
- Small tubes of colored icing in bright colors
- Colored sugar sprinkles

★　✳　★　✴

1. Bake the cupcakes according to your recipe. Make sure to ask an adult for help with the oven!

2. Once the cupcakes have cooled, use a spatula to spread frosting on the top of each cupcake.

3. Using the little tubes of icing, draw a big star on top of the frosting on each cupcake.

4. Add colored sugar sprinkles to your cupcakes. (You can also use star-shaped sprinkles, if you can find them!)

Now your cupcakes all have colorful, sparkly stars on top—just like the stars Cassie sees when she and Stella fly through the night sky!

Can Cassie make another wish come true?

Take a sneak peek at

#5: Wish Upon a Superstar!

✷ 1 ✷

Strawberries and Sparkles

Suddenly, the silver light burst into thousands of tiny sparkles that swirled toward Cassie. With a *whizz* and a *fizz* and a *zip-zip-zip*, the sparkles gathered into a column of light.

"Hi, Stella!" cried Cassie, running to hug her.

"What a nice welcome," Stella said in her soft, warm voice. "And what pretty strawberries."

"Try them!" said Cassie, holding out her basket.

Stella chose a strawberry. "It's heart

shaped!" she said. Then she tasted it. "Mmm, delicious!" She touched Cassie's bracelet with her wand. "Do you like your new cupcake charm?"

"It's great," said Cassie, "but I don't know what power it has. Can you tell me?" she asked. "Or maybe give me a clue?"

Stella raised her wand above Cassie's head, and bright light shone down from it.

Cassie felt like she was standing in a spotlight! She twirled like a ballerina. "Do I look like a star onstage?" she asked, laughing.

Stella smiled. "Not everybody enjoys being in the spotlight, Cassie." She winked.

Was that a clue?